Run For S

Written and Illustrated by: Patrick Johns

Sometimes Kevin would wake up early and see his mom go out for her morning run.

One morning, Kevin decided to join his mom for a run. He tried to get his brother Matt to go too, but Matt said he didn't like to sweat.

Kevin liked the feeling that running gave him.
He felt energized.

Soon he began going out running on his own.

Kevin noticed on the days he would run, the weather would always end up being very nice. He bragged to everybody that he could control the weather by running.

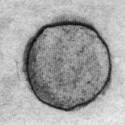

Nobody believed him at first, but then the town started doing research. On the days that Kevin ran, it would always be sunny and nice out.

On the days he did not run, it would rain or be a tad chilly.

They also discovered that the longer Kevin ran,
the nicer the weather would be.

Pretty soon the word about Kevin's running spread around town and the requests began. Mrs. Davis asked Kevin if he would run for her because she was having a family picnic.

Kevin's baseball team always made sure that he ran on game days. No more rain-outs!

Ms. Anderson asked Kevin to run on Sunday because she wanted to plant her flowers on that day.

The town's mayor wanted Kevin to run a very long way because the town was having a parade and he wanted the conditions to be absolutely perfect.

Pretty soon, Kevin was running a long way every day
to make everybody happy.

One day, Kevin felt very tired and did not want to run.

A lot of the townspeople got upset and demanded that he run.

Kevin's mom told them to leave Kevin alone. This angered the townspeople.

"If he doesn't run, there's going to be trouble!" they yelled.

Kevin and his mom went inside. The townspeople began banging on the door. "Come out and run!" they yelled.

Kevin, Matt, and their mom sat at the kitchen table and tried to figure out what they should do.

Kevin jumped up and shouted, "I have a plan!"

The door opened and Kevin came out.
"Go run!" ordered the mayor.

Kevin began to run and then something strange happened...

it started raining...

"It looks like Kevin does not really control the weather with his running," said the mayor.

"Go home Kevin."

Kevin went back into his house....

But it actually wasn't Kevin at all. It was his brother Matt in disguise!

Kevin's plan had fooled the town! Now he would be able to go running whenever he wanted. Hooray!

Made in the USA
Lexington, KY
15 January 2014